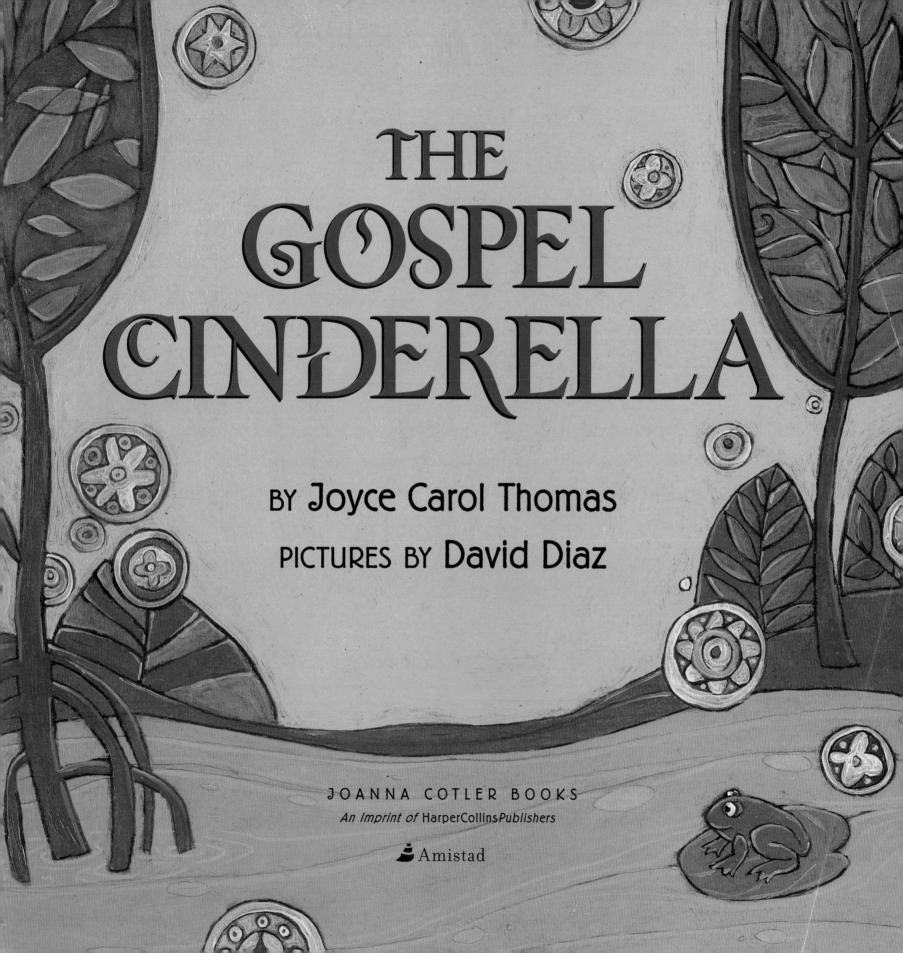

THE GOSPEL CINDERELLA

BY Joyce Carol Thomas

PICTURES BY David Diaz

JOANNA COTLER BOOKS
An Imprint of HarperCollins Publishers

Amistad

O nce upon a time, Queen Mother Rhythm, leader of the Great Gospel Choir, lived deep in the swamp with her beautiful baby daughter. In a voice as flavorful as licorice, she sang lullabies to her darling child.

One day, right after Queen Mother Rhythm had sung her baby to sleep in her basket by the river, a hurricane came up out of nowhere. It knocked Queen Mother Rhythm off her feet and swept the sleeping baby downstream out of reach and out of sight.

After the hurricane had blown over, Queen Mother Rhythm looked high and low, but she could not find her baby girl. She searched weeks and months, but still she never found her child.

And through the years, when Queen Mother Rhythm led the Great Gospel Choir in concert, her voice was always thick with sorrow and joy. Sorrow over the loss of her child and joy over the blessed relief she found in the music.

From a cup set before me I sip sorrow each day Every time I swallow I find sorrow's come to stay Then flavors of joy I taste in my cup

It so happened that way on the other side of the swamp, Crooked Foster Mother lived in a ramshackle cottage with her twin baby girls, Hennie and Minnie.

After the hurricane, Crooked Foster Mother found a basket washed up on her shore. Inside the basket there was a little baby covered with mud after being swept down along the swamp for days and days. But she was peaceful, cooing like a fine-feathered songbird.

"I sure don't need another mouth to feed," Crooked Foster Mother said, "but what I could use is another hand in the kitchen." She picked up the basket and carried the baby home. "And seein' how you're as dirty as a cinder pile, I guess I'll call you Cinderella."

Now Crooked Foster Mother was so evil that even the sun was scared to rise when she was outside. And as the years passed, Hennie and Minnie grew to be just as mean as their mama. The three of them made Cinderella do all the work around that old ramshackle cottage. They made her do the cleaning, the sewing, and the cooking. Every day Cinderella had to make ten sweet potato pies and ten pots of collard greens, which Crooked Foster Mother and the twins ate all up. They never left Cinderella anything but the pot liquor from the greens.

Cinderella never complained, though. She just went about her chores cheerfully humming and happily singing, which made the twins and their mama even meaner. They hated to hear Cinderella sing because her voice just seemed to get stronger and truer as time went by, while all they could do was croak like swamp toads.

Meanwhile, back on the other side of the swamp, Queen Mother Rhythm decided it was time to find a new lead singer for the Great Gospel Choir. "I'm ready to retire," she told her piano-playing Prince of Music.

"I'll find somebody to take your place, Queen Mother Rhythm," said the handsome Prince.

And the Prince of Music had his Royal Runners run up and down the swamp, sticking flyers on trees and hanging them on bushes. They ran to the east. They ran to the west. They ran to the north. They ran to the south.

When Cinderella picked up one of the flyers announcing the audition, she longed to try out. She longed to be a Daughter of Rhythm. But Crooked Foster Mother had other plans.

"My two daughters got rhythm!" Crooked Foster Mother announced, snatching the flyer out of Cinderella's hand. "Cinderella, you will teach them a song they can sing at the Great Gospel Convention."

Oh, it was hard. Hennie and Minnie had sour voices. And try as Cinderella might, they still sounded awful.

After a whole day of listening to Hennie and Minnie messing up the music and singing the notes whop-sided, Crooked Foster Mother got so mad, she chased Cinderella through the kitchen, knocking over pots and pans. She chased her right out of the house, past the chicken coop, where poor Cinderella crouched, trembling in fear.

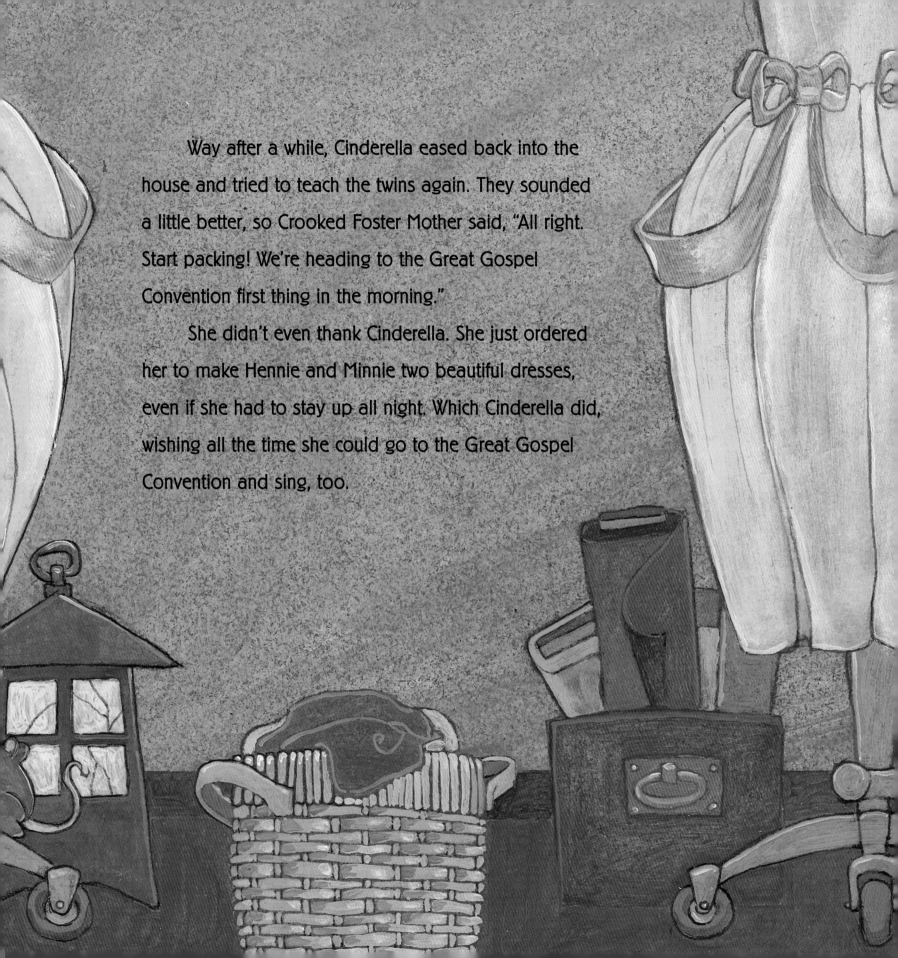

Way after a while, Cinderella eased back into the
house and tried to teach the twins again. They sounded
a little better, so Crooked Foster Mother said, "All right.
Start packing! We're heading to the Great Gospel
Convention first thing in the morning."

She didn't even thank Cinderella. She just ordered
her to make Hennie and Minnie two beautiful dresses,
even if she had to stay up all night. Which Cinderella did,
wishing all the time she could go to the Great Gospel
Convention and sing, too.

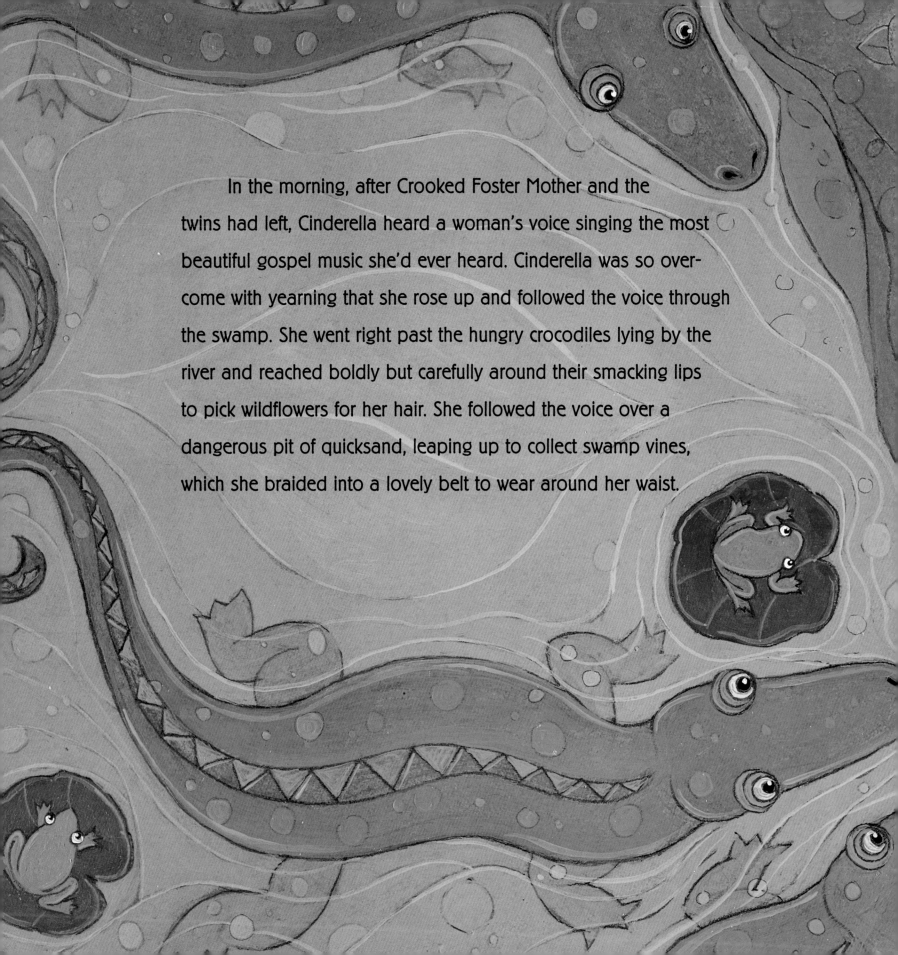

In the morning, after Crooked Foster Mother and the
twins had left, Cinderella heard a woman's voice singing the most
beautiful gospel music she'd ever heard. Cinderella was so over-
come with yearning that she rose up and followed the voice through
the swamp. She went right past the hungry crocodiles lying by the
river and reached boldly but carefully around their smacking lips
to pick wildflowers for her hair. She followed the voice over a
dangerous pit of quicksand, leaping up to collect swamp vines,
which she braided into a lovely belt to wear around her waist.

Cinderella followed that voice, winding through the swamp
until she reached the Great Gospel Convention. By now she was so
disguised by the plants and flowers she had found along the way
and made into a costume that not even Crooked Foster Mother and
the mean twins could recognize her. But Cinderella stayed at the
edge of the crowd just in case.

Queen Mother Rhythm sang the opening number with such spirit that the rhythm rocked the trees.

We have called a great gospel convention

All these singers have come from miles around
When we hear that golden voice
We're sure to recognize the sound!

There were all kinds of groups who sang. Choirs from the north, quartets from the east, trios from the west, duets from the south. But still, after listening closely to every one of them, Queen Mother Rhythm would look at her Prince of Music sitting playing the piano and shake her head no. They did not have the voice she wanted.

When it came their turn, Hennie and Minnie sounded so terrible, they got booed by the crowd and ran back to their row, where they scrunched low in their seats.

Crooked Foster Mother was so upset, she mumbled to herself, "Wait till I get ahold of that Cinderella. I'm gonna wring her neck!"

But Crooked Foster Mother wasn't the only one upset. Queen Mother Rhythm still hadn't found her new singer—and the convention was almost over.

It was just about then that Cinderella got up enough nerve to sing. She started from way in the back of the audience and sang her way to the front. The Prince followed her song on the piano, loving every note of her gospel voice.

Cinderella's sound was so gentle and bold that people hushed and stood up and craned their necks to see the girl who enchanted them with a voice as sweet as licorice.

Tears of joy rolled down Queen Mother Rhythm's cheeks as she listened to the beautiful voice sing the words she knew so well. She looked at the Prince of Music and nodded her head yes.

Never missing a beat, the Prince gazed deep into Cinderella's eyes, and Cinderella felt her heart begin to soar along with the notes she was singing. The minute Cinderella finished her heavenly tune, the whole crowd went crazy, clapping and cheering.

But before Crooked Foster Mother and the twins could recognize her, Cinderella turned around and fled. She ran back through the swamp, back past the quicksand, where she left the belt of vines, back past the crocodiles, where she left the wildflowers, and back into the ramshackle cottage.

"We heard her, but we lost her," said the Prince to Queen Mother Rhythm back at the convention. "Now I must find her."

The very next day, the Prince of Music and his Royal Runners began to search all up and down the swamp. They went to the north, they went to the south, they went to the east, they went to the west.

"Why don't we give up?" said the Royal Runners. "We'll never find her."

But the Prince of Music said, "Let's keep going," and they pressed on, disturbing screech owls, wildcats, and resting raccoons.

Finally, they came to Crooked Foster Mother's cottage.

"We need to hear everybody in your house sing," the Prince ordered.
Crooked Foster Mother was evil, but she wasn't crazy enough to disobey
Gospel Royalty.

"Just a minute," she said to the Prince. Then she hurried outside where
Cinderella was cleaning the chicken coop and handed her a toothbrush. "Here,
use this to paint the henhouse. And don't come inside till you're finished!"

Back with the Prince, Crooked Foster Mother lined up her two no-singing
daughters. They sang so bad, they made the Royal Runners' ears ache.

The Prince sighed and headed for the door. But just as he was making his way toward the river, he thought he heard someone humming a familiar tune. He followed the sound until he found Cinderella behind the henhouse. He stood quietly listening, and Cinderella's voice seemed to make everything around her sparkle with an enchanted light.

"Finally, we have found our singer!" the Prince exclaimed, and the Royal Runners came running, with Crooked Foster Mother and the twins close behind. Crooked Foster Mother and the twins were so upset, they started squawking like mad hens. But the Royal Runners shushed them up, wanting to hear the perfect duet Cinderella and the Prince were singing.

When the Prince of Music brought Cinderella back through the swamp, Queen Mother Rhythm listened again to the golden voice and knew deep in her heart that Cinderella was her long-lost child.

"You are my own true Daughter of Rhythm," Queen Mother Rhythm sang out loud. Now that her sorrow had been wiped away, every word she spoke came out in sweet melody.

And so Cinderella took her rightful place beside Queen Mother Rhythm and the Prince of Music, singing and leading the Great Gospel Choir.

For Aurora Pecot, with love

—J.C.T.

For Gabrielle

—D.D.

Amistad is an imprint of HarperCollins Publishers, Inc.

The Gospel Cinderella
Text copyright © 2004 by Joyce Carol Thomas
Illustrations copyright © 2004 by David Diaz
Printed in the U.S.A. All rights reserved.
www.harperchildrens.com

Library of Congress Cataloging-in-Publication Data
Thomas, Joyce Carol.
  The gospel Cinderella / by Joyce Carol Thomas ; illustrations by David Diaz.
      p.   c.m.
  "Joanna Cotler Books."
  Summary: A variation on the traditional Cinderella story set in a Southern
swamp and with a Great Gospel Convention instead of a ball.
  ISBN 0-06-025387-8 — ISBN 0-06-025388-6 (lib. bdg.)
    [1. Fairy tales.   2. Folklore.]   I. Diaz, David, ill.   II. Title.
PZ8.T364Go   99-42905
[398.2]—dc21   CIP
                                                               AC

Designed by David Diaz and Alicia Mikles
3 4 5 6 7 8 9 10
❖
First Edition